In memory of my mother, an inveterate duck-feeder ~ M.C.

For Jenny Reeve ~ R.R.

We're Going to Feed the Ducks copyright © Frances Lincoln Limited 2003
Text copyright © Margrit Cruickshank 2003
Illustrations copyright © Rosie Reeve 2003

First published in Great Britain in 2003 by
Frances Lincoln Limited, 4 Torriano Mews
Torriano Avenue, London NW5 2RZ

www.franceslincoln.com

British Library Cataloguing in Publication Data
available on request

ISBN 0-7112-1961-3

Set in Layout Regular

Printed in Singapore
9 8 7 6 5 4 3 2 1

We're Going to Feed the Ducks

Margrit Cruickshank ⊚ Illustrated by Rosie Reeve

FRANCES LINCOLN

We're going to feed the ducks!

Look! What a friendly brown dog!

No! We're not going to feed
the friendly brown dog.
We're going to feed the ducks.

Look! **TWO** squirrels with bushy red tails!

No! We're not going to feed the squirrels
with bushy red tails.
We're going to feed the ducks.

Look! **Three** cheeky little sparrows!

No! We're not going to feed
the cheeky little sparrows.
We're going to feed the ducks!

Look! **Four** fat pigeons!
Listen to them go *prruuu, prruuu, prruuuuu!*

No! We're not going to feed
the fat noisy pigeons.
We're going to feed the ducks!

Look! **Five** squabbling seagulls!
Aren't they rude!

No! We're not going to feed
the rude squabbling seagulls.
We're going to feed the ducks!

Oh, all right then. We'll toss a few crusts
to the **five** squabbling seagulls.
There you are, seagulls!

We might as well give the
four fat pigeons some too.
There you are, pigeons!

And the **three** cheeky little sparrows.
I suppose we can spare them a few crumbs.
There you are, sparrows!

Do you think the **two** squirrels
will eat out of our hands?
There you are, squirrels!

The friendly brown dog's begging!
We'll have to let him have a slice as well.

Now we can feed the ducks!

Oh! Sorry ducks.
The bread's all gone!

All right. We'll get you some more.

We're going to feed the ducks!